Sharmela McLaughlin

Living for a moment

Sharmela McLaughlin

Living for a moment

when two hearts meet

JustFiction Edition

He seemed satisfied with that and just nodded.

Brian and Ria had been absolutely no help throughout the entire lunch, she reflected as she took her last sip.

*****

Angel didn't hear from Brad in the days that followed, nor did she expect to hear from him again, considering she hardly talked at all on their date but he surprised her three weeks later with a call on work.

"I got your office number from Brian."

"Okay."   Angel didn't know what to say to him.

"I hope you don't mind."

"No...ofcourse not."

"Honestly I've been buying time to call you," he confessed.

That revelation made her smile.   "Okay," she said again.

"I know you probably can't be on the phone long at the office.   Can I call you on your house number after work?"

"Ummm....I guess."   She really didn't know what to say to him and God alone knew why she gave him her number.   Now she had to look forward to another awkward call.

*****

Rain was falling, the pitter patter of raindrops on her window was a mild distraction as she delved into *Bag of Bones* a recent Stephen King novel.

"*I went to Manderley again.*"   That haunting line from the book gave her goose bumps but she loved it.   She could envision the log cabin in the woods where the character once shared with his deceased wife.   So entralled by the story, Angel didn't hear the phone ringing in the hallway.

"There's some guy on the phone for you!"   Her sister announced with her hands posed on her hips and a look of suspicion in her eyes.

"Okay."   Angel didn't offer any explanation as she went to answer.

"Good night my Angel."

She was taken aback by his greeting, not sure weather to be impressed or worried by his slightly possesive tone.   Brushing her thoughts aside she responded politely.

"Good night."

"Do you have a radio close by?"   He questioned.

"A radio?"   She thought that was such a weird question.

"There is one somewhere..."

"That's great. I want you to turn it on and listen to 95.1, I sent in a request to play for you," he informed.

"Oh..."   Angel was speechless.

"I just called to tell you that," he said softly.   "Good night my Angel."

Angel held the phone in her hand momentarily, allowing what he said to sink in before finding the radio and turning it on.   And at that moment she heard the radio announcer say, "This song goes out to Angel, coming from Brad who's sitting aboard the MV Splash thinking of you.   Its Lenny Kravits - Again.   And Brad is wondering if he'll ever see you again."

It was the most   romantic gesture, she had ever experienced and it touched her heart more than she expected.

*****

Calling her every evening became a tradition, which Angel was quickly getting accustomed to.

"Why do you let him call you so much?"   Barbie didn't hide the irritation from her voice.

"I don't know...because he likes to."   Angel shrugged her shoulders.

"But do you like him to?"   She questioned.

"I don't have a problem."

"You normally don't like anyone calling you.   Why him?"

"I don't know.   All we talk about is world views and politics.   Nothing for you to get all flustered about."

"I just hope you're not falling for him."

"No...of course not."

        "He's not good enough for you."

"Now how can you say that!   You don't even know him," Angel got defensive.

"I know enough to know he's not good for you.   For one he's too old, second he's divorced and third he's a captian on a boat.   He probably has a girlfriend on every port!"

"That's stereotypical.   He could be different."

"He's divorced!   Doesn't that say something?"

Angel shrugged her shoulders dismissively.

"What about our plans to visit France, and fall in love in Paris?"

"When will we ever go to Paris?   That's just a fantasy."

"I can't believe what I'm hearing!   He's brain washing you with all those calls!   I hate him!" Barbie shouted before storming off.

Angel sighed deeply, not understanding why everyone seemed to be against the idea of Brad and her.   Tammy insisted that she just wasn't getting the vibe so to speak and her sister kept saying he wasn't good enough for her.   Her parents too, had a problem with him calling everyday.   It was just a few harmless calls but they were all acting as though he were some sort of serial killer.

*****

"What does this Brad and Angel have to talk about so?"   Her mother's voice was far from casual as she sliced through the juicy tomato.

Barbie took a huge gulp of orange juice so she wouldn't have to answer and shrugged her shoulders instead.

"Angel said that you guys met him at one of the concerts you went to at Pier 1.   What does he look like?"   She questioned, her eyes sharp and inquisitive.

Barbie almost choked, the juice spluttering from her mouth as she coughed in an effort to catch her breath.   She was going to strangle Angel for this.   She had never even seen the man and now she had to describe him to their mother.   Their mother was Jewish and she wanted Jewish husbands for them.   She had her own match making plans instored for their future.

"You can tell me.   I won't get angry."

Barbie resisted the temptation to laugh.   Her mother's friendly facade was thin and she knew she had to tread carefully.

"What can I say?   I hardly noticed him.   All I know, they exchanged numbers."

"You must have gotten a glimse of him!"   Her voice was no longer calm.

Sure I have lazer eyes that can see straight through people's minds, she thought

6

sarcastically.   Angel was going to have to pay for this, big time.

"He was not very attractive.   Angel didn't like him.   I really don't know why she gave him her number,"   Barbie hoped she sounded convincing.

"That relationship is not going to work," her mother continued.   "Him being offshore all the time.   What kind of marriage would that be!"

Barbie's head snapped up.   "Who said anything about marriage!"

Her mother did not answer.

"Mother, they're just talking. The man probably gets lonely on the boat. Imagine just having a radio for company."

"He's only messing with her mind. I've to put a stop to this."

"Good luck with that," Barbie answered before leaving the kitchen.

She ran headlong into Angel in the hallway.

"Mum wants to know if you're gonna marry Brad!"

"What!"   Angel asked incredulously.

"You heard me."

"Everyone's going insane."

"You're the insane one.   No one likes the man.   Just end it."

"I don't have to listen to this -"

"Look I'm sorry," Barbie apologised.   "Make him call less, that's all."

Angel nodded before retreating to her room while Barbie went downstairs to feed the canary.

"Was that the American again?"   Her father had the bird out of the cage, walking on the ledge.

Great, not you too, she thought.

"I think so."

"It's better you girls go to France. Walk in your grandfather's footsteps."   He seemed to be talking more to himself than her.

Barbie didn't comment but returned upstairs to tell Angel what their father had just said, hoping that the minor guilt trip would help her to see things more rationally.

"I see," was all Angel said in an expressionless voice.

7

*****

"I think I'm falling for him."

Tammy stopped entering data on the computer.

"And I think, you're not."

"How can you say that?"

"Because I know you.   You're just settling for him."

"I don't agree with you."

"That's because you're too stubborn to admit that I'm right."

"You are not," Angel said with determination.

"Angel you don't even know him.   Talking on the phone is not the same as spending actual time with the person.   You haven't been out with him since that blind date and you want to believe you're falling for him?   That's ridiculous!"

"We'll meet at some point and I think we'll get along just fine."

"Honey, you've known him for two entire months and you haven't met yet.   Doesn't that tell you something?   Perhaps God doesn't want you guys to meet."

"Please don't get all spiritual on me," Angel rolled her eyes.

"Maybe it's not meant to be," Tammy continued.

"You're starting to sound like my sister."

"Something keeps preventing you guys from meeting.   I would take heed if I were you."

"Tammy, you're not being helpful," Angel exclaimed.

"Well let me ask you one question before I rest my case."

"Be my guest."

"What about travelling to Europe and finding the love of your life in Paris?"

"That was just a fantasy."

"But what if you had the opportunity to do that?   Would you be satisfied with Brad?"

"That's two questions."

"You haven't answered."

Angel opened her mouth to protest but nothing came out.

A moment later Tammy spoke softly.   "There...you have your answer.   Your silence speaks volumes.   I am right."

Disturbed, Angel rose from her seat without meeting Tammy's eyes.   "Thanks for making me feel awful," she said gloomily.

"You know you value my brutal honesty."

Angel nodded with a disheartened expression as she returned to her desk.

CHAPTER 2

Monday morning staff meeting was always a dilemma.   Mr. Davis the Project Manager always had his hands full when it came to giving directives but this morning was an exception.   He did not have to deligate any new projects as he announced the closing of the financial year.   It was an election year which meant that the Ministry of Local Government were shutting things down early so members could focus on campaiging for elections.

Even though the closure of the office had been looming in the air for some time, it still came as a hard blow for Angel.   They could not have chosen a worst time to shut things down. Just when things were starting to brew between she and Brad, she was being sent home to prison.   She knew that once she was not working, she would not be able to get out to see him, if the opportunity arose.

Feeling despondent, she went through the emotional task of hugging staff members. With their contracts terminated, no one was certain to come back for the new financial year. Angel loved politics and working in that environment but sometimes she wondered if the uncertainty was worth it.   Finding another job that was not influenced by political affiliation would provide more stability but she loved interacting with the people within the constituency and trying to help make a difference in their daily lives.

She cleared out her desk before taking a taxi down to the library, not in the mood to go home right away.   While there, she tried to read hoping to distract herself from her current situation but she could not concentrate.   Too many things were on her mind.   She was over thinking again, a habit she just could not shake off.

Ria showed up unexpectedly, just when she had shut the book.

"What's up chick?"

Angel shrugged her shoulders dismissively.   "How did you know where to find me?"

"Coincidentally I happened to get the same taxi you left with and I asked him where you stopped off."

"Oh," was all Angel managed to say.

"I came to cheer you up.   I spoke to Brian a few minutes ago and he said that Brad wants to meet up with you."

"Really?"   Angel was dubious.

"Really!"   Ria smiled.

"When?"

"Like now!"

"Are you serious?"

"They're waiting for us at Kim Far."

"Jeez I'm not even prepared," Angel protested.

"Let's just go!"   Ria exclaimed.

The atmosphere at Kim Far Restaurant and Lounge was relaxed when they entered. Brad and Brian were sitting at the far end.

"We finally meet again," Brad was cheerful as he pulled back the chair for her.

Angel smiled in response.

A waiter came over with the cocktail menu.   Angel spanned the extensive list before deciding on a Strawberry Daiquiri and Ria followed suit.

"It's so great to see you," Brad held her gaze.

Angel smiled, trying not to blush.

"I have the day off tomorrow.   Can you spend it with me in San Fernando?"

She was not expecting that.   "I -"

"Yes she will!"   Ria answered for her.

Angel threw her a sideways glance of slight annoyance.

"I have a meeting in the morning but then I'm free for the rest of the day.   How about Gulf City Mall?   Want to meet up around eleven?"   His voice was optimistic while his brown eyes searched her face.

Angel took a deep sip of her drink.   " I guess..."

"That's wonderful!"

*****

She avoided thinking on the drive up because she was afraid to place high expectations, however he was waiting there when she arrived.   They greeted each other with a hug before he took her hand and led her through the mall towards the Gallery Pub which was the only place open at that time in the morning.

There were not much people about but the few followed them with curious eyes.   Angel hated to imagine what they were thinking.   The pub was empty except for two men drinking.

Brad ordered a Carib beer for himself and she took a coke.   The bar tender had an odd expression as he handed them their drinks and Angel silently wondered what kind of picture

11

she and Brad portrayed.   Probably not a great impression, she decided.   After all she was sitting opposite a man, almost twice her age and the difference showed.

Brad had told her on the phone the previous night that he had something important to tell her but he wanted to say it in person.   Her sister speculated that he might propose while she was expecting him to ask her for a serious relationship.   What he told her, however was so far fetched from what she expected that she was momentarily speechless.

"The thing I couldn't tell you on the phone last night is this..." he spoke slowly, his big brown eyes searching her face.   "I have a girlfriend."

At first Angel thought he was joking or just saying that to see her reaction but then she realized he was serious.

"Is she in the U.S?"   Her voice surprisingly did not crack or quiver inspite of the shock.   There were a hundred things storming through her mind.

"No.   She's Trinidadian from Union Village."

Another local girl, Angel thought as she took a sip of coke and swallowed hard.

Brad continued talking nervously.

"She's in her mid - thirties with two kids and I've only known her for three months.   I met her last October on Brian's birthday at the bar where she works," he explained.

"What's her name?"   Angel did not know why she asked or what difference it would make.

"Sandy."

"Do you have an intimate relationship with her?"

"Yes," his voice was low as he shifted uncomfortably on the seat.

Angel wanted to escape but she did not know how.   Instead she took a sip of coke, silently wishing it was a beer.   She surpressed a sardonic laugh.   Who else would find themselves in this postion? Only her!

"Do you call her everyday like you call me?"

He nodded.

Now she really wanted to scream or just disappear.   If she could evaporate into thin air like some migician whe would feel relieved.

"When was the last time you saw her?"   The ability to ask that in a calm voice, surprised her even more.

"Sunday."

That was the day before he met up with her and Ria at Kim Far restuarant.   She was disillusioned big time.

Brad continued to talk but she half heard him.

"I never meant to hurt you.   Since I've met you, I've thought about no one else.   I've been contemplating forever whether to tell you or not but in the end I just wanted to be honest with you."

Angel mustered all the inner strength she could find to respond to him politely.

"I'm glad I heard it from you instead of finding out from Brian or someone else," she managed to say.

"Do you have a boyfriend?"

"No."

"How come?'

She shrugged her shoulders.

"I didn't want to hurt you.   That's the last thing I wanted."

She nodded before looking away from him.   "Are you going to end the relationship with her?"
"Is what we have going to become something?"

"I don't know," she answered flatly.

"Brian and Rufus are telling me that I shouldn't let you slip away."

"Who is Rufus?"

"My best friend over here. You'll meet him today, he'll be driving us around."

She stared at him silently thinking that she wanted to go home right at this moment.

"Brian and Rufus prefer you for me," he continued.

"Why?"

"Because you're innocent and I can trust you."

"How would you know that?"

"Angel I've been in town since June last year and I've never seen you.   No one knows anything about you but everyone knows Sandy at the bar where she works!"

"You checked up on me?"

"Yes," he answered honestly.

Angel didn't know if to feel annoyed or impressed by that.

"What if you do the same to me? Suppose you meet someone else down the line?"

He shook his head in denial. "When you find something precious you don't let it go."

He was full of all the right words, she thought sarcastically. "Are you going to end the relationship with her?" She asked again.

"I think I'm probably just going to blow it off."

"But that might hurt her." Was she really advocating for the other woman? In the end she did not want to be the reason for anyone's pain.

"I know, but you're the one I don't want to hurt."

"You're just saying that."

"I'll never lie to you."

"I don't know if I can trust you," she said without emotion.

"I understand but I'm willing to earn your trust again. As long as it will take. I will do anything for you," his voice was earnest.

She looked away from him again

"Let's go for a walk," he changed the subject.

They left the Gallery Pub silently, each absorbed in thoughts of their own. He tried to hold her hand and she involuntarily tensed.

"Now you don't want to hold my hand."

"You can hold my hand if you want," her tone was flippant and he took the hint.

There were more people in the mall now and everyone kept looking at them. They headed to Hi -Rpm, another pub within the mall but it was closed so they stood outside on the balcony.

"What are you thinking?" He asked.

"Nothing."

"Say what you feel Angel," he pleaded with her.

"I've stopped thinking," she answered.

"No one can do that. We're always thinking."

She had the ability to zone off, she was good at that. She was an expert at disassociating and letting her mind trail off some where else.

"Please tell me what you're thinking."

"Nothing. I'm just enjoying the breeze against my face," she responded as she leaned further into the railing.

Desperate to break the silence he began telling her funny stories about his family.   At first it just sounded like rambling but she found herself smiling after a while.   She could never resist a good sense of humor in anyone and it was one of the qualities that drew her to him.   It was easy to forget his age when he started talking and he had a knack for making her laugh.

"Let's go to Celeb's," he told her.

She nodded as she followed him back into the mall.

There were free foutune cookies outside Celeb's Pub and they each took one.

His fortune told him that he needed to do better investments while hers said that she needed to be alert.   They both laughed at that.

"Are you going to drink a Carib this time?"

"No I need to be alert," she joked.

"One should always be alert."

"But I probably need to be extra alert today!"

They both laughed at that.

After they settled with their drinks inside, he gave her a picture of the MV Splash, the million dollar vessel he lived on.   She studied it with mild interest before listening to him talk about his family once more.   His son, she learned was just two years older than her.   He was probably the one that should be sitting opposite her, she thought but then again she was mature beyond her age.   Someone at twenty two might not understand her. She had such an old soul.

"Are you hungry?"   He asked when they had finished their drinks.

"No."

"Let's take another walk."

He tried to hold her hand again and this time she let him.

"What would you like to get?"

"Nothing."

"You're still upset huh?"

"No."

He walked into a jewellery store and tried to buy her an expensive diamond studded watch but she refused.   She did not care about material things.   She wanted a relationship based on honesty and trust, one where true love was the foundation.   They ventured into a few more shops before going outside to wait on Rufus who was picking them up.

They were there for less than a minute before Rufus pulled up, accompanied by two TT Coast Guards.

"Do you have your driver's liscence?" Brad questioned.

She nodded.

"I'll buy you a car. What kind do you like?"

Angel did not bother to answer him.   When he realized she was not impressed he changed the conversation.

"Where would you like to go?"   He asked.

Some where nice and quiet like San Fernado Hill, she thought to herself.   "It does not matter," she replied.

"How about San Fernando Hill?   I've been up there twice and its very beautiful."

She was surprised at their parallel thinking but did not say.

Rufus came out of the van to greet them.   "How are you beautiful?"   He hugged her as if he had known her forever.

"I'm good," she smiled, instantly drawn to his easy going nature.

"When's the wedding?" He teased.

Why she blushed at that, she did not know.

On the drive over to another bar, Rufus kept   looking back at them mesmerised.

"Bars, bars and more bars," she muttered under her breath.

"You don't like?" Brad questioned.

She shrugged her shoulders.

They pulled up at Jenny's on the Boulevard and took a private table at the back.

"So when is the wedding? Next week!!" Rufus was cherry.

Living for a Moment

"Will you be best man?"   Brad asked seriously.

"Any time you're ready.   Even tomorrow!"   His voice was laced with excitement.

They talked about what size of ring would fit her finger and Angel listened without saying anything.   They continued to make wedding plans as if she were not there and just when she was about to protest, the conversation changed to investment deals and prospective business ventures Brad could consider to start for his life on the island.

Angel silently noted, that he had a good head for business with the potiential to be successful. *And the rich becomes richer* was the quote that popped into her mind.

"Are you going to marry him?"   One of the coast guard questioned when he saw that she was losing interest in the conversation at hand.

"I don't know," she replied honestly.

"What do you mean, you don't know?"   He seemed surprised by her answer.

That's a foolish question, she thought but did not say.   For an esteemed coast guard she expected better.   She meant exactly what she said.   How complicated was that answer?

"I'll take you guys to a nice hotel," Rufus suggested.

"We prefer to go to the Hill," Brad stated.

"Do you know what Rufus was implying?"   Brad whispered next to her.

"Yes but I don't believe in sex before marriage," she answered bluntly.

"And I would never put you through that," he said gently.

"Where in Trinidad would you like to live?"   Brad asked after a while.

"I never thought about that," she anwered feeling a downcast shadow descend on her.   She was going to fall in love in Paris and live near the French Alps where she and her better half could go skiing in the middle of a snow storm.   She had never seen snow but knew that she would love it. That's where she had planned on living.

"I want you to think about it," he broke into her train of thoughts.   "Wherever you want to live I'll buy a house. Think of your own home with your own rules!"

Angel said nothing, torn in two directions - the dreams of her past and all that Brad was promising.

They finally pulled up at the base of the hill.   Clean mountain air blew against her face as she climbed down from the van and Angel filled her lungs.   They followed a winding track that led to the top and then stood to stare at San Fernando City below them.

17

"Very beautiful," he commented.

She nodded, taking in the view but he was looking at her.

"Angel?"

"Ummm?"   She met his brown eyes.

"Will you marry me?"   He was searching her face.

Angel looked away, guiltily.

"You don't have to answer me now.   Think about it but I'm not going to ask you again."

      Angel remained silent.

"Marriage is not about love," he continued.   "It's about being compatible.   Love will come after."

"How would you know if we're compatible?"

"We are. I'm mellow and you're quiet and we get along," he reasoned.

Angel did not say anything.

"Please think about it," he urged.

She nodded, not wanting to give him any false hope.

Taking her hand, he led her back down the hill to where the van was parked.

      "You're so innocent and sweet," he commented as he opened the door for her.

Angel, resisted the impulse to roll her eyes.   "I'm not a child."

"No, you're not.   You're a baby."

She could not help smiling at that.

*****

"How was your day?"   Barbie asked with disinterest.

"Good.   I had a nice time," Angel was deliberately evasive.

"What did he have to tell you?"   She didn't waste time beating around the bush.

"You're very curious."

"Fine, you don't have to tell me!"

      "He proposed just like you said he would!"

18

"And you said no, right?"

"I told him that I would think about it."

"But you're going to say no. Are you?"   She finished uncertainly when Angel did not respond.

"I don't know. I'm going to give it serious consideration."

"I can't believe what I'm hearing!   Just tell him, no!"

"What is the problem?"

 "I don't want to be related to the man!   Don't expect me to come to your wedding!"   Barbie stormed off.

        Brad called almost immediately after, providing the perfect diversion.

"Just called to let you know that I'm thinking about you.   I miss you already."

She remained silent.

"Angel?"

"Yes."

"I want you to think seriously about everything."

"I need time."

"I know you do.   You're young and beautiful and it's an important decision...but please give it serious thought."

"I will."

"Angel?"

"Uh huh?"

"I love you."

"You don't know me."

"I know all I need to know.   I've been around the world and I've never met anyone like you!"

"There are loads of people like me," she chided.

"Darling, you're one in a million."

Angel hung up the phone, smiling at his compliment.

CHAPTER 3

Two weeks later en route to the shopping mall Angel and Ria took a short cut off Adventure Road, however before they could get to their destination Angel noticed Brad on the balcony of Casablanca, a newly opened pub.

"Look, there's Brad," she said surprised pointing in his direction.

"My God he's drunk!"   Ria exclaimed.

"It seems so."

"Let me go and get him," Ria stated.

Ria called out to Brad from the bottom of Casablanca's stairs.

Brad   came down but he was not alone.   A woman was latched unto his arm.

"Hey Ria!   How ya doing?"   He asked before turning his attention to the girl glued to his arm. "Sandy, this is Ria.   She's the one who introduced me to Angel.   How is Angel by the way?"

Ria stood there dumbfounded.

"Brad doesn't want anything to do with Angel," the girl said stonily to Ria.

"Angel doesn't love me.   Sandy lovs me!   She showed me just how much last night, didn't you babe!"   He said before kissing her.

With uncertain eyes Ria looked over their shoulder to see Angel standing there. She had witnessed everything.

Angel didn't expect to be hurt but she was. She could feel her heart sinking from her chest to the bottom of her soul as she turned and walked away, her eyes filling with tears. She did not undestand how she could instantly be consumed by such greif when she wasn't in love with Brad. She was only fond of him. She could hardly see the pathway to walk as tears gushed from her eyes.

Ria caught up with her. "Angel I'm so sorry."

Angel nodded unable to find her voice. She felt so dillusioned by everything. She would never find love she concluded. It only existed in her imagaination, and even that she was unsure about now. Emotionally she was so distraught, she did not know how she was ever going to trust someone else now.

Angel continued walking, feeling neither here nor there. "I'll be okay," she spoke sofly trying to console herself but somehow she did not feel convinced. A lonliness she had never felt began to wash over her entire soul and she felt like she was reaching saturation point really fast.

"Angel please talk to me," Ria tried to reach out to her.

Angel just shook her head. She couldn't talk, her voice was lost somewhere in the depts of her throat.

*****

Angel reached for the jar of sugar and absently took out a spoon to sweeten her traditional morning coffee.

"Wrong bottle, that's salt," her mother pointed out.

Angel blinked in an effort to focus. "Thanks," she answered distractedly before replacing the lid on the salt bottle. She was in no mood to drink anything, nor was she in a mood to listen to her mother relate her on the argument she had had with her father twenty minutes ago. Her parents were forever fighting and if she wasn't used to it by now she would never be. Her mother ranted on while she struggled to keep an interested face.

Can't you see I don't want to listen mother? Her mind screamed. I've got enough problems of my own without having to sympathize with yours, she thought in frustration. She realized her usually expressionless eyes betrayed her thoughts from her mother's next words.

"What's on your mind?"

Angel blinked without saying anything.

"Is it your job?   You shouldn't worry too much about it.   They'll call you back."

Angel remained silent.   Her job was the last thing on her mind.

"Why don't you and Barbie go by Dianne for a little holiday?"

Angel's eyes lit up with surprise.   "Do you mean that?"

"Sure I do. It'll take your mind off the closure of work."

"Thanks mum," Angel hugged her.

Angel really needed the diversion. She felt as though her entire world had fallen apart in the blink of an eye and she desperately needed to get away.   She was feeling trapped with each passing moment, the walls closing in around her.   Her lonliness and pain was eating away at the core of her being and she did not think she could take any more.   She had reached saturation point, her system completely filled.   She couldn't feel anymore after feeling too much. Her relationship with Brad had impacted her so much that his departure had pulled the rug from under her feet, letting her freefall all the way down into an abyss she couldn't seem to climb out from.

Angel blinked hard, snapping herself out of her daze.   The time for reminisincing was over.   She had to move on.   Brad no longer belonged in her presant nor her future.   She did not want him back nor did she want anyone for a long, long time.

"We're almost there," Barbie announced.

Ten minutes later Dianne was showing them into her appartment.

"How are you holding up?"   She directed her question to Angel.

"Good, inspite of it all."

"You look so thin.   Are you eating?"   She asked with concern.

"Not much but I'm getting there," Angel assured her.

"What about you Barbie?"

"I'm good too," she responded quickly making everyone laugh.

"How long will you be staying at your in laws?" Angel inquired.

"Just a couple of days. You know where everything is.   Can you light the stove?" She teased.

Angel smiled.

"Don't burn the down the place," she teased again.   "And remember to lock up properly if you girls decide to go out."

"Don't worry, everything will be okay," Angel assured her.

"Do you have any plans?"

"Not much.   Barbie wants to go to Hi-Rpm tomorrow night but I'm not sure what we're going to do."

"As long as you're careful and don't lose the keys," she added.

Angel and Barbie laughed at that.

*****

"When are you going to get dressed?"   Barbie questioned with her hands posed on her waist as usual.

"Dressed for what?"   Angel did not remove her eyes from from the television screen.

"To go Hi-Rpm duhh!"   She threw her arms up in the air.

"I'm not sure we're still going."

"What do you mean you're not sure!"

"If this movie doesn't finish by half seven I'm not going anywhere.   It will be too late!"

"Nonsense!   This is something we've always wanted.   Now is our chance.   We have a whole night of freedom!   This might never happen for us again," Barbie stressed.

"I'm not in the mood," Angel returned despondently.

"Get in mood!   Black Rose is playing.   That's your favourite band!   What's wrong with you? We went quite Port-of-Spain to see them perform and here they are right under our nose for free and you have second thoughts!   That's absurd!   Forget Brad," she added.

The mention of his name made Angel feel worse.   How long was she really going to sit around moaning over him and getting increasingly depressed while he was probably having fun with Sandy at that very moment.   Barbie was right, she should go out and enjoy herself.

"Fine, we'll go after this movie."

"That's the spirit,"Barbie praised.

An hour later they were on their way from Marabella town down to La Romain where Hi-

"It's okay," she replied.

"Is it okay or good?"   He questioned.

"It's good," she smiled.

"Good. Every where I go I keep hearing soca. I'm fed up. I want some rock music!"   He was being honest with her.

Even though she loved rock music, she was disappointed that he didn't like local music. Most tourists usually loved it.   Steve continued to talk but her mind trailed away again.

"I'm sorry.   What did you say?"   She asked when she realized he was waiting for an answer.

"I asked if you would like something to drink?"

"Ummm...coke."

Steve tried to make polite conversation but she kept spacing out.   He snapped his fingers infront her face bringing her back to earth.   She tried to apologise with a smile but did a feeble job.   She was forcing herself to have a good time but it just was not happening. After a while Steve gave up and joined Yhan to sing, while she sat on the stool he vacated absorbed in her own thoughts.

Barbie joined her on the stool next to her sipping a Malta, when Curtis the lead singer of Black Rose came over to shake their hands and tell them thanks for coming.   He did recognise them after all.

"How are you girls getting home deep South?" Ross asked close to closing time.

"We're staying at a friend's place in Marabella."

"That's cool.   Royal Hotel where these guys are staying is close to Marabella.   We can give you a lift."

"Okay."

"Is it safe to go with them?"   Barbie questioned.

"I'm not sure," Angel admitted.   "Let's be safe."

"Sorry Ross.   We've changed our minds about the lift."

"Look these guys are not looking for trouble.   You don't have to be afraid."

"It's not that.   We're staying a bit longer."

He shrugged his shoulders after a while.

Angel and Barbie waved at the group as they took their leave before they went in search for their own taxi to Marabella.

*****

Dianne returned to the appartment around six a.m when Angel had just gotten up.

"Had a rough night?"   She raised curious brows.

"Something like that," Angel answered in a tired voice.

"You look like you can sleep the entire day," she commented.

"I think that's what I'll do.   Just wanted to eat something first."

"Where's Barbie?"

"Still asleep.   She'll probably get up tonight," she quipped.

"How was Hi-Rpm?"

"The band was good and we met some Belgians."

     "Oh really?"

"Yeah but we didn't really connect."

"Better luck next time," Dianne laughed.

     Angel nodded as she pried open a can of sussage before emptying the contents on the grill and cracking an egg over it.   She didn't have the energy for much else.   Sitting in front the television she picked at the food while she stared at the screen distractedly.   Her mind flashed back to the night before.   The highlight of the evening had been Black Rose, everything else was swaddled in disillusionment.

     The Belgians who should have resonated with her because of their proximity to France and the French culture, didn't connect with her which was a big disappointment. Silently she wondered if she would ever find someone who would truly understand her.   She felt so alone and didn't know how she was going to get through this phase.

     Last year around this same time love and companionship was the last thing on her mind. She was only concerned about working and having fun going to different concerts and events. Essentially she was just enjoying her life and doing things her way.   She never wanted to meet a significant other and those she met she pushed away.   She was used to walking alone and she liked it but now somehow she was different.

     Her experience with Brad had changed her in more ways than she could account for and for once she didn't want to be alone. She needed someone to take her in their arms and make a feel safe, she wanted a special person to care for her and make her laugh again.   She wanted someone to help her forget everything that was hurting her at the moment.   But there was one problem...she didn't think she could trust anyone again.

Emotionally, she felt like she was drowning and needed someone to extend a hand to reach out to her but there was no one who understood her enough.   Brushing away the tears that trickled down the side of her face, Angel switched off the telvision before emptying her food in the garbage.   She had no appitite.   Feeling like she had reached the end of her rope, she crawled back into bed and welcomed the oblivion of sleep.

CHAPTER 4

"Homeward bound tomorrow," Angel said noncommitally.

"So where are we going tonight?"

"I don't know but definately not Hi-Rpm.   I didn't enjoy myself at all."

"Neither did I," Barbie agreed.   "Maybe we can check out Mystic 16 in Chaguanas.   I heard over there rocks."

"Not a bad idea except we don't know where it is."

"No problem.   We'll just tell a taxi to take us there."

"We can't keep taking chances like that.   One day we might not be lucky," Angel said seriously.

"That's one day away and not today," Barbie said without restriction.

Angel gave her an annoyed look before switching on the TV and flipping through the channels, settling for MTV's top ten countdown when she did not find anything interesting to watch.

"What are you girls up to?"   Dianne asked coming out of her bedroom with a frown etched upon her face.   "I just had the most disturbing dream," she siad distractedly.

"What was it about?"   Angel asked without removing her eyes from the screen.   **Backstreet Boys - The Call** was playing and it consumed her attention.

"I dreamt that you and I were the only two people who didn't get called back out to work."

"That's just your subconscious mind playing games with you."

"It feels more like a premonition.   Why haven't the ministry called as yet?"

"Don't worry in advance," Angel tried to distract her.

"I'm going to give Tammy a buzz to see what she's heard."

"Grapevine information is not going to help," Angel pointed out.

"Tammy usually have good sources," Dianne insisted as she picked up the phone.

Angel half lended an ear to their casual greetings and small talk.   **Match Box Twenty's -**

If you're Gone was more interesting.

"What do you mean work started today!"

Now that remark got Angel's attention.

"Who got called out?   What happens to us then?"   Dianne's voice was laced with panic.

Angel didn't have to hear Tammy's end of the conversation to realise what was happening.

Dianne hung up the phone with an expression of doom and gloom.   "They started work today," she said flatly.

"Why would they start at the end of the week?"   Angel asked.

"It's the Ministry of Local Government.   If they're not back to front then it wouldn't be them!"

"Okay calm down.   There's no need to panic."   Angel could tell that Dianne's cool was slipping away.

"Tammy said that there are five more people to be called out on Monday but she can't tell if our names are on the list."

"There's still hope then," Angel tried to be optimistic but Dianne was still agitated.

"Maybe if you see Anthony you'll feel better," Barbie treid to help.

"Good idea.   What time does his shift start at **Mc Donald's**?"   Angel was glad for the diversion.

"He's there now," Dianne said with a sigh.

"Let's all go down. We'll eat some Ice-cream and chill lax," Angel smiled.

The atmosphere at **Mc Donald's** was relaxed.   They all sat down eating soft served Dairy milk ice-cream before Dianne made her way back to the appartment in Marabella and Angel and Barbie boarded a taxi down to Hi-Rpm.

When they arrived, the Belgians were already there, standing footsteps away from the entrance.   Angel recognized Steve and stared at him for a moment thinking that he looked good.   She had not paid much attention to his appearance on the first night but now she realised he was a rather attractive man.   He looked like a carbon copy of Ben Affleck, only with blond hair and blue eyes.

As though sensing her eyes on him he looked in her direction.   He recognised her right away and came over to hug her.

At the same time Barbie noticed one from the group that she liked and asked Steve if he could call him over.

"Who?"

"The tall blond one with the hair," she emphasized.   "He's talking to the Rasta man!"

"That's Ken," Steve told her as he tried motioning him over but the Rasta man had his undevided attention.

Yhan came over and reached for Angel's hand before kissing it.   She knew that was a French tradition but supposed it was a Belgian one too since they all did it on greeting.

Steve held on to her and she allowed herself to relax in his arms.   She had every intention on enjoying herself tonight.   The prospect of not having employment was pushed to the back of her mind.   She tried not to think as she danced in Steve's arms, getting increasinly comfortable by the minute.   As the night grew on he held her closer and Angel did not protest. She did not realise how much she needed to be held until now and by God she did not want him to let her go.   She did not care that he was a perfect stranger whom she knew nothing about and she was not concerned whether he was attracted to her or not.   All she wanted was to remain enclosed in the affectionate embrace of his strong arms.

He rubbed his masculine jaw against her face, his stubble grazing her skin and making her think of a wheat field in winter.   With half closed eyes he brushed his nose against hers affectionately and Angel was awed by the gesture.   She could see desire reflecting in the blue depths of his eyes, which looked almost gray in the dim lighting of the club.

He blew warm breath into her left ear and it surprised her when her entire body broke out in goose bumbs.   Her body seemed to be responding to him with every fibre of her being.

"I want to kiss you," he said huskily, rubbing his face against hers once more.

"I'll think about it," she whispered.   Her voice had retreated somewhere in the back of her throat.

Steve held her tighter, caressively stroking her arms in a soothing motion while his stubble continued to graze the side of her face and neck once more.   Her body continued to respond to him like a magnet that found its polar attraction and Angel did not fight it.

When his head finally came down and his warm lips claimed hers, it seemed like the most natural thing in the world.   Hugging her towards him he drew her towards the counter to sit on a bar stool.   She nesstled between his legs, leaning against him.   Steve continued to rub his face against the sensitive skin on her back and shoulders, blowing warm breath into her ear and sending shivers down her spine.

Angel couldn't believe what was happening.   Her body seemed to belong to him and was responding on its own against her will. Her mind wasn't functioning anymore but every cell in her body seemed to be awakening in his arms.

His moist tongue began to suck on her earlobe, tugging at the loop of her earing and the hairs at the back of her neck stood on their end.

"Stop making love," a girl said as she fitted herself next to them to order a drink over the counter.

Angel did not realize that the girl had spoken to them until she repeated herself giving Angel a sideways glance.   Angel ignorned the remark, turning her face towards Steve as he planted a kiss on her neck.

Ken the tall blond guy who her sister was interested in passed at that instant, almost tripping over Steve's boot.   Angel looked at him and smiled with a devious glint in her eyes.

"You did that?"   He looked over his shoulder with a smile.

Angel shook her head in denial, watching as he came over to lean against the counter next to she and Steve.

"Steve's my brother," he told her, his blue eyes dancing.

Angel smiled but did not believe him.   He was obviously toying with her.

"He really is my brother," Steve smiled before kissing her neck again.

Ross the driver came over and informed that he was making a trip to the Royal Hotel. The entire group left but Ken and Steve remained.

"We will go when you return for the next trip," Steve told him.

"Can you take us to Marabella?"   Angel questioned.

"Wherever you and Steve discussed," Ross said.

"We didn't discuss anything," Angel said firmly.

"I'll take you guys to the hotel then."

"No we can't go to the hotel," Angel said seriously.

"Then I'll go over to your place," Steve teased brushing his lips against hers.

They left the club and went for burgers across the street where there was a line of carts selling street food.   By the time they had finished eating Ross returned but the car was almost filled with Venezuelans.

"Come on you guys can still fit in," Ross urged.

Barbie sat on top of Ken while she sat on top of Steve, thinking if their mother only knew she would strangle them alive.

The radio was playing **White Snake's - Here I go again** and together she and Steve sang at the top of their lungs.

Ross pulled up at Royal Hotel.   "I have to drop these Venes off.   I'll come back for you girls after."

It was against Royal Hotel's policy to have unregistered guest in any room but they talked to the guard on duty who wavered a bit and let them into Steve's room which was on the ground floor.

Once inside Ken lay down on the bed and Barbie took her place on top of his chest staring down into his blue eyes which was so much like his brother's, idly parting his blond hair which fell over his forehead carelessly.

"You remind me of Dawson and I feel like Katie."

"I think I saw Dawson's Creek once.   He's a good looking guy right?"

That comment made her laugh.   "You're so sweet," she said fondly, still playing with his hair. "My John Smith."

Angel and Steve on the other hand were flipping through the channels, the limited amount available, with little success in finding anything of interest.

He tried to hold her but she withdrew.

"It will be just like Hi-Rpm, nothing more," he assured her.

"Okay," she said softly, allowing him to take her in his arms.

"You're a serious girl," he told her after some time.

"What do you mean?"   She asked thinking not him too.   She was accustomed to people telling her that she was too serious and needed to smile more.

"You're a good girl," he amended.

"Is that a compliment?"   She asked uncertainly.

He nodded before brushing his lips against hers.

As soon as they turned off the lights and were about to settle in, Rodney the security guard came pounding at the door.

With no other choice the foursome made their way out front to sit on a low concrete wall.

Barbie sat on Ken, savoring the moment while Angel sat next to Steve, allowing his arms to keep her warm from the cool ticklish night air.

"You're a good guy," Angel told him.

Steve remained silent.

"There are not many guys like you.   You're a really nice guy," she finished honestly.

A small silence passed between them.

"If I gave you my number, would you call?"   For some reason she did not want it to end.

"Would you be able to come and meet me if I did?"

Angel thought about it for a moment.   She thought about returning deep South Trinidad, about her over protective parents, her traditonal Jewish mother and all the barriers she would encounter and heart sinkingly she knew it was a dead end.

"No," she answered softly.

Another moment of silence descended upon them, each absorbed in their own thoughts.

Ken flicked a lighter close to the side of her face making her jump while he and Barbie bubbled over with laughter.

Ken and Steve lit up Benson and Hedges but the smoke aggravated her lungs making her cough uncontrollably.

Steve flicked the cigarette away before rubbing her back gently.   Angel was silently touched by the gesture.

"There is cancer in all of us," Ken teased.

"Oh really?"   She cleared her throat.   "Then that includes you," she teased him back.

A Canadian guy stood close by with his luggage and Ken flicked his cigarette butt over the guys's head but the Canadian remained oblivious and Barbie giggled hysterically at Ken's antics.

"Do you want to go over to the bar to get something to drink?"   Steve asked.   "It will help to get the smoke out of your lungs," he continued when he saw the reluctance in her eyes.

"But all those people are going to look at us," she protested, her eyes wavering over the filled tables, all with Canadian men eating their breakfast.

"So what?"   Steve was unmoved.

"Okay," she relented.

Angel settled for a coke, while they had their traditional Carib Beer and Barbie took a Malta which they repeatedly say until they got the pronunciation right.

"You guys work for Dredging International?"   Barbie questioned.

"Yes, but really a company called SMITE," Ken said spelling it out for her.

"We work for two weeks before we're allowed one day off and that's when we go Maracas," Steve informed.

"We've never been to Maracas," Angel told him and thinking at the same time that, it seemed like forever since they had been to any beach.

"You've never been to Maracas?"   Ken asked surprised.

They both shook their head in denial.

"The next time we have a day off, we'll take you to Maracas," Steve said seriously.

Yeah right, Angel thought.   After today you're never going to see us again or visa versa.

The conversation moved on to movies, **The Blair Witch Project**, popping up.

"I saw the movie but I wouldn't have understood it, if I hadn't read the book," Angel explained.

"You read the book?"   Steve asked surprised.

She nodded.

"I hate to read.   I don't have the patience for it," he stated.

"Were you afraid when you saw the movie?"   Ken asked.

"Nope," Angel answered.

"Not even a little?" He raised blond brows in surprise.

"No," she insisted.

"Not even after you saw them running through the bushes?"

At that they all dissolved in laughter.   Ken had obviously gotten a good scare from the movie.

The conversation then diverted to Europe.   They mentioned Ibiza, explaining that it was a party island with beaches along the Mediterranean sea.

"We've always wanted to go to Paris.   French is such a romantic language," Angel commented.

"I worked in Paris for six months and never spoke a word of French," Steve informed.

"For six months?   What did you speak then?"   Angel was curious.

"English," he laughed.   "I hung out with English students and workers."

"I went up Eiffel Tower,"   Ken announced proudly.

"And what did you do? Fall Down!"   Steve teased making them all laugh.

"It's very high and eveyone was upside down from on top," Ken defended.

"Is that your purse?"   Steve asked lifting it from off the chair.

"That's what it's like in Turkey," Ken commented.   "It's a normal thing there.   You rest down your bag and the minute you turn your back it's gone so fast," he continued, mimicking the way it happens and making everyone dissolve in laughter again.

Angel and Barbie were enjoying their sense of humour so much that before they knew it, day break had dawned and the morning sunshine began filtering into the room.   The night had disappeared so fast and none of them had slept.

"You guys have to work soon,"Angel commented with concern.

"We will be alright," Ken said.

"We have to leave..."   Angel said reluctantly.

"Would you like us to walk you out?"   Steve asked.

"Yes," Angel smiled, silently touched by the gesture.

He leafed his arm around her waist drawing her towards him as they made their way down hill from the Royal Hotel.   Ken and Barbie followed suit.

They waited for a few minutes before a taxi eventually pulled up.   Steve brushed his lips affectionately against hers.   "See you in Hi-Rpm sometime?"   His blue eyes were optimistic.

Angel nodded with a smile.

The brothers stood at the foot of the hill waving them off as the taxi departed.

"They are so sweet," Angel and Barbie said in unison.

CHAPTER 5

"I want to see them again," Barbie said.

"So do I, but it's hopeless," Angel replied.

"We've got to come up with a plan," Barbie insisted.

"You know that's not going to get us anywhere," Angel said in a defeated tone.

"Do you want to see Steve again or not?"   She asked in exasperation with her hands posed traditionally on her waist.

"I do."

"Then don't look at me, start thinking.   Let's put our collective minds to work!"

"How about just letting her know we went to Hi-Rpm?"

"Like that is going to work!   She'll kill us," Barbie threw her hands up in the air.   "You know our mother is not open minded!"

"I have an idea!"   Barbie exclaimed after a while.   "Let's tell her Friday is band night."

"How is that going to help?"   Angel asked with a blank expression.

"Hello!"   Barbie snapped her fingers.   "We go all over to see bands perform and here it is right under our nose."

"I guess you have a point."

*****

"No," their mother said firmly.

"Come on mom please..." Barbie begged.

"What about No, don't you understand?"   Their mother asked with a tinge of impatience.

"You allow us to go quite Port-of-Spain to see the same bands, why can't you allow us to go right Gulf-City?"   Angel tried her luck.

Going to concerts once in a while is different from going to a club on Friday night!"

"I don't see the difference.   It's the same kind of people, the same music, just in an enclosed area," Barbie insisted, gesticulating with her hands.   "It's even safer than a concert because at concerts there's the mosh pit where people act real wild!"

"What kind of reputation do you girls want to have?   How will you get good husbands when they find out you go clubbing on Friday night!"

"Jeez mom!   What era are you living in!   This isn't Bible days!"   Barbie threw her hands up in the air.

"Mother we're adults!   People that go to the clubs are younger than us!"   Angel persisted.

"My final answer is no and I don't want to hear about this again!"   Their mother stormed out of the room.

"I told you this was going to be useless," Angel said defeated.

"I'm going to talk to dad."

"Why bother?   He's going to be worse."

"I'm not going to give up.   I want to see Ken again."

"Well good luck with that."

*****

"I can't believe we're actually on our way,"   Angel said softly as she stared through the window of the maxi taxi into the darkness outside.

"I told you they would come around.   Gulf City is only an hour away.   Compared to Port-of-Spain, this is in our back yard."

"Now all we have to do is meet them again..."   Angel mused.

"Hopefully we will," Barbie said in a wistful tone.

They arrived at nine o' clock and found themselves a table at the back to relax.   Sipping coke they just took in the laid back atmosphere and music.

About half an hour in, Greg a guy from deep south who knew them waltzed over to their table.

"You girls want company?"

Angel shrugged her shoulders.

"Who are you girls waiting on?"

"Some friends," Barbie interjected.

"It's almost ten, maybe they're not coming again.   You girls could join me on the next side with some friends.   They're really cool."

"No thanks, we're still gonna wait," Angel said.

"Still?"   He seemed surprised by that answer, his eyebrows rising high on his forehead.

"Well you can't say I didn't offer," he smiled before taking his leave.

By half ten he was back with one of his friends.   "This time I really don't think your friends are coming.   We hate to see two beautiful girls just sitting by themselves."

Angel was really beginning to think the same even though she remained expressionless.

Barbie however made no attempt to hide her irritation and was about to tell them to take a hike when she noticed Steve and some of the group.

"I think Steve is here," she said loudly.

Angel gave her a look that told her to stop playing games.

39

"No he's really here," she said and Angel followed the direction of her gaze.

"I'm sorry," Angel began to apologise to Greg.

"It's okay," he said awkwardly as he watched them go.

When Steve saw her he took her hand and entwined his fingers with hers. "We have the day off tomorrow and we're going to Maracas. Do you want to go?"

She smiled, her heart warmed by the gesture.

"I've got some bad news too."

She raised enquiring brows.

"I wouldn't be off for Carnival," he said disappointed. "I have to work. What are you going to do?"

"I'm staying at home. I don't participate in Carnival."

"You don't?" He seemed genuinely surprised. "You're the first person I've met to say that."

Angel shrugged her shoulders dismissively. Carnival was usually a few weeks before Passover and even though her mother was Christian now, she could not help being Jewish. It was in her blood. All High Holy Days and traditions were kept in their house but she did not tell Steve this.

"Where is Ken?" Barbie wasted no time to find out.

"Still at the hotel. He wasn't feeling too well. I don't know if he went to sleep but when he's asleep you could drop a bomb and he wouldn't get up."

"Oh man," Barbie said disappointed.

"Is there a phone around? We could try calling him," Steve suggested.

"There's a phone booth downstairs," Barbie said eagerly before they went to find it.

They did not succeed in getting through to Ken, the phone in his hotel room just kept ringing.

Barbie whined in disappointment, making Steve laugh.

As they were about to ascend the stairs back into the club a guy came over to tell Steve that some girl across the street was calling him.

Angel followed the direction the guy was pointing before looking back at Steve.

"Is she your girlfriend?" Angel could feel her heart sink to the bottom of her chest.

Steve shook his head in denial. "I don't know her."

"She seem to certainly know you," Angel tried to keep the sarcasm out of her voice but didn't exactly do a good job.

"Are you going to see what she wants?"   Angel asked.

Steve nodded uncertainly.

At that moment Angel needed to be reassured.   It was so difficult for her to trust anyone after what happened with Brad.

Steve entwined his fingers with hers.   "Let's go and see."

Together they crossed the street to where the girl was.   It tuned out that Ross, their driver was her boyfriend and she was trying to locate him.   Relieved at that, they returned to Hi-rpm to join the group, most of which had arrived by then.   They were all standing close to the stage but Angel didn't like that location because of the bright lighting.

"Why did they have to stand here?"   Steve asked as if reading her mind as he drew her close to him.   Hugging her tight they swayed to the music.

"What's wrong?"   He asked in a concerned voice after a while.

"Nothing."

"You look so sad," he told her.

She was really losing the art of keeping an expressionless face.   She was once so good at that.

Steve gently placed her head against his chest, in a comforting gesture, patting her affectionately.   His kindness and gentleness made her even more emotional and she shruggled to hold back the tears.   This complete stranger was being so affectionate, it was enough to reduce her to tears.   The last thing she wanted was to be a burden to him.   Burrying her face, deeper into his chest, she blanked her mind of all thoughts.   She was tired of over thinking.

His hand accidently raised the bodice she was wearing and she pulled it down in an attempt to fix it.   The second time it happened he pulled it down for her, making her smile in spite of everything.   He playfully rubbed his nose against hers before his moist tongue reached out to lick her lips.

Angel was uncertain about what was happening and even more uncertain of how to respond to that.

"Are you okay?"   He asked again.

She nodded but he still placed her head back on his chest affectionately, making Angel hug him tighter.

Shaggy and Raven's song *Angel*, started playing and Steve stared down at her, singing it to her and that action got her emotional.   She closed her eyes fighting back the tears.   He was too sweet.   She was wrong for him.   He deserved someone he could have carefree fun with during his limited stay on the island.

"I'm very tired.   It was a difficult day at work.   I really need to rest."

Angel nodded.   She could see how drained and flushed his face was.

They left the group to return to Royal Hotel but Glen the security guard on duty was adamant that they could not go into the room.

The instant Glen turned his back, Barbie hurried up to room 218 to find Ken, who got up sleepily after two knocks to open the door.   He was surprised to see her but stepped aside to let her in, before locking the door behind them.

Barbie took out her sandals before going to lie on his bead as if it were the most natural thing in the world to do and Ken joined her after.

"How was Hi-Rpm?"   He asked from deep within his throat.

"Good," she answered turning towards him on the bed.

"I'm not well," his voice was soft.

"Poor baby," she murmured affectionatly stroking the side of his face before a loud pounding knock sounded at the door.   It was Steve informing them that the guard was searching for her. With no choice Barbie left the room with Steve to join Angel downstairs.

They walked out to the front of the hotel where Olivier and Mitus were swearing in Flemish after the taxi had ripped them off by charging tripple price.   Ross arrived shortly after with his girlfriend and another guy called Dane.   Dane looked Belgian but his Trini accent was a dead give away.   Angel and Barbie warmed to him naturally.

"You guys can crash by me, down in Bel Air," he offered.

They agreed to that as they piled into Ross's car.

"See you in Maracas tomorrow!"   Olivier waved to them.

Dane's double bed did not seem big enough to fit all four of them.   Angel and Steve occupied the middle, spooning like penut butter and jelly in a sandwich while Barbie and Dane were on either side.

Steve fell asleep almost immediately with his head resting against her breast, his weight pinning her down and making her immovable.

Dane who seemed restless got up to turn on the radio.   One of Angel's feet chose that specific time to start cramping and she winced in pain while trying to nudge Barbie to get up and help her.   How she could sleep with the radio so close to her head, bewildered Angel and didn't help her situation.

"Dane as you're up. Can you pull back my toe?   My foot is cramping really bad."

"Just throw his leg off and you'll be okay."

Angel groaned as the contractions increased.   She must have been groaning louder than she thought because Steve got up to rub her foot, massaging it expertly.

"The veins are rubbing against each other," she moaned trying to explain.

"I know," he said gently.   "It happens to me sometime when I play football."   He continued to massage her foot until it stopped cramping.

They settled back down on the bed, Steve placing his head on her belly and she gently ran her fingers through his hair while he slept.

"You can't sleep can you?"   Dane voiced next to her.

"No," there are mosquitoes zinging by my ear."

"I'll fix that," Dane said getting up.

Angel suppressed the urge to laugh at his remedy which consisted of a mixture of aftershave and cologne which he poured into the oscillating blade of the fan, filling the room with the sweet masculine smell.

Barbie who wasn't asleep after all starting giggling beside her and then they all dissolved in laughter.

"If you can't sleep, we can talk," Dane said returning on the bed.

"Is that your book?"   Angel asked referring to the novel on his night stand.

He nodded.

"Sidney Sheldon is a brilliant writer," she commented.

"You've read his books?"   He questioned with interest.

"Some of them."

"I just finished this one. "

"Tell me your Dreams," she read the title.

"You can have it."

"Really?"

He nodded before handing it to her.

She talked with Dane until the wee hours of the morning before finally difting into a light

43

sleep.   Sunlight flitering into the big bay windows woke her up.   Dane was snoring softly next to her and Steve's steady breathing against her neck indicated that he was still asleep.   No movement came from Barbie's direction and Angel guessed she was asleep too.

She shifted to make herself comfortable and the movement made Steve hold her tighter, drawing her closer to him.   She snuggled up in his warmth, thinking so this is what it's like to wake up with a man.   He was holding her affectionately even in his sleep and she was filled with a sense of wonder.

It was her first experience of being in bed with a man and just the prospect of it was outrageous, yet she was not uncomfortable.   If anything she was a little too comfortable for her own good.   More than anything she wanted him to continue holding her in the way that he was.   For once she felt safe and protected.   Like someone cared, even if he didn't.   At some point in life one needed the comfort only a man could give and visa versa.   Their situation reminded her of war and how strangers seeked comfort in each other's arms in their quest for survival while they were hundred of miles away from their families - just living for each moment.

She looked at his sleeping figure next to her before kissing his forehead lightly.   She wondered if he had a wife and kids waiting for him back in Belgium...or a girlfriend perhaps.   She did not expect such a verile man to be single.   Thinking about it, she realized she hardly knew anything about the man in whose arms she had found all the affection she had ever yearned for.   He could be an ex convict for all she knew.   Even his last name was still a mystery to her and yet it did not matter.   They were living for the moment, concerned only about the here and now and that was all that mattered to her.

One of Dane's baby pittbulls came into the room before climbing unto the bed, waking Barbie in the process who got up to play with him.   Angel laughed as she too patted him and the commotion woke Dane who pushed him off the bed.   That didn't deter the pup who tried to climb back up again.

Steve opened his eyes sleepily and laughed when he saw the pup.

"He wants attention," Dane said as he dropped on the floor to lie with the pup.

"How did you sleep?"   Angel asked turning to Steve.

"Very good," he responded before brushing his lips against hers and drawing her closer to him to bury his face against her neck.

Angel idly played with his soft blond hair as he nuzzled against her.

After a while she got up to use the bathroom but couldn't get the faucets to work.

"Are you a tourist?"   Dane teased.   "You can't work our Trini pipes?"   He laughed as he turned on the shower for her.

When Angel returned she sat at the foot of the bed.

"Come on, there's no need to be shy.   This is where you spent the night!   Feel free to lie down again," Dane teased.

Steve smiled when she returned next to him, wasting no time to draw her in his arms to cuddle up against him.   He kissed the bridge of her nose and smiled when he saw her taken aback expression before kissing her lips.

Angel wrote about such things but she never expected them to materialise in her world. She kissed him back not protesting at first when his hand started to trail up her leg.

"Tell your hand to behave," she murmured against his lips.

"It's not listening," he responded, smiling as she wriggled away from him and out of his reach.

Barbie was about to enter and Dane pulled her hand leading her out. "Give them some privacy."

They didn't need it, Angel mused as she returned next to Steve on the bed.   He enveloped her against him again.

"What's your last name?"

"Damion."

"Damion?"   She questioned surprised.   She was expecting a long Flemish name, she wouldn't be able to pronounce.

Some time later they went with Dane to find breakfast but there was no where opened so they settled for Doubles, a popular Trini street food before walking half a mile to find a phone box to call home.

Dane assured them that Ross would come later to pick them up but knowing from experience that Ross was not the most reliable person they took a taxi back to the Royal Hotel.

Steve made it back just in time as the maxi was about to depart for Maracas.

He hugged her close before kissing her.   "See you again in Hi-Rpm sometime?"

She nodded while Barbie waved out to Ken who was sitting at the front of the maxi.

Then they boarded a taxi home.

CHAPTER 6

Angel slowly walked away from the office with the mid morning sun beating down on her but she hardly noticed.   She was heading to the Techier Community Park to spend her lunch period.   No one was there when she arrived and she crouched beneath a tree, enjoying the shade and cool breeze.   She was glad to be alone, this was the type of solitude she liked and savored.

Her mind absently flittered over to Steve and she wondered how he spent his day at Maracas.   She wondered too how it would have been if she and Barbie had went with them.   Sighing she deliberately pushed him out of her mind.   She did not want to think too much about him because she could not afford to get attached since they were leaving soon.

She stood up before walking over to the iron swings and sitting down on one.   She rocked back and forth, absorbed in her own thoughts as the wind blew through her hair.   She was a child at heart but she had such an old soul that most people didn't understand her. Only the day before the site supervisor on the La Brea project, wanted to know her age and when she questioned why he told her that he was curious because she exuded a been there, done that aura.   She had smiled at the compliment not sure if it was a blessing or a curse to be that way.

Glancing at the time on her watch, she realized she had to head back to the office.   She got up and straightened her suit before exiting the park.   The only thing that brightened her mood as she walked back to the building was the prospect of seeing Steve later at Hi-Rpm.

*****

"I had the most terrible day," Barbie complained as she plunked down on the sofa.

"What happened?"

"Look at my poor fingers, they're sore from typing on that old type writer!   And he only let me have five minutes to eat my lunch!"

"That's really bad," Angel admitted.

"I came this close to quitting," she emphasized with her thumb and index finger.   "Cheapskate lawyer!"

"It might get better in the future," Angel tried to encourage.

"I'm too young for this kinda stress.   I just want to see Ken this evening."

Angel smiled at that.   "Not long ago I was thinking I just want to see Steve too."

"Collective minds again!   We must be twins," Barbie laughed.

*****

Dane kept them company when they arrived.

"Can I get you something to drink?"

"Malta," they said together.

"You girls are old ladies!   I'm not buying drinks without alcohol for you.   Shandy is only two percent alcohol," he said before ordering two.

"I've just been to the hotel.   I saw your boyfriend Steve," he smiled at Angel.

She was taken aback by his statement.   She had not realized that he considered Steve to be her boyfriend.   She wasn't sure what he was to her or her to him.   She had avoided thinking about anything and just went with the flow.

"I saw him strutting his tattoos," he told her with knowing eyes, as if she knew.

She didn't know though, she had never seen his tattoos.   She was not even aware of them but Dane obviously thought she knew.   She supposed that was because he had seen them sleep so intimately at his place the week before.

"Are they coming tonight?"   Barbie asked.

"Her boyfriend, Steve is coming.   He told me that he'll be here for sure."

Half an hour later Olivier and Mitus joined them but Angel was beginning to wonder if Steve had changed his mind about coming.

He unexpectedly showed up twenty minutes later and wasted no time to take her in his arms.   Angel hugged him back, filling her lungs with the masculine smell of his aftershave as she pressed her nose against his neck.

Barbie watched as Steve rubbed his nose against her sister's adorably and as though sensing her eyes on him, he looked up and smiled with her before returning his attention back to Angel.   He was so sweet, she was glad that Angel had finally found someone that she liked and who seemed to like her just as much.   Ken on the other hand was ignoring her and she sat down on one of the bar stools with a plump.

"Do you want to go outside?"   Steve asked about an hour later.

Ross handed him the car keys and Angel noticed Olivier and Mitus watching.   She knew what they were thinking.

"Your friends are going to think I'm sleeping with you."

"Again!"

His statement made her laugh.

"I don't tell them anything but even if I did, they wouldn't believe me," he said   leading her to sit on one of the benches outside the mall.

He kissed her lips before trailing kisses along her neck and then nibbling on her earlope.

"It's not right," she protested.

"With you, it's never right," he smiled.   "I'll have to marry you first?"

"Yes," she said seriously, making him laugh.

"Dane mentioned that you have tattoos."

He nodded.   "Do you want to see them?"

She was surprised by the offer and nodded uncertainly.   She watched as he removed his T-shirt.   She was not used to seeing a half naked man and had to fight herself from blushing as her eyes roved over the wide expanse of his chest and muscled arms and shoulders.   He had an eagle on his arm and a unicorn on his left shoulder.   She resisted the impulse to touch him but ended up doing so in spite of her inner objections.   She could feel his blood vessels contract and vibrate beneath her fingers as she traced his tattoos and   was silently amazed that his body was responding so intensly to her touch.

"We should go back up," her voice was husky.

He nodded as he put back on his T-shirt.

They returned to find Ken and her sister dancing with a crowd encirled around them. They were putting on quite a show and Steve hugged her between his legs as they sat down to watch them.

"Do you have a girlfriend back in Belgium?"

Angel didn't know what made her ask.

He was silent at first but then nodded hesitantly.

Angel remained silent, absorbing the new information.   It did not surprise her, she was somewhat expecting that.   Part of her wondered if it was better not knowing at all.

Steve rubbed her shoulders affectionately, in a comforting gesture and she pushed the thought of his girlfriend, somewhere half way across the world in Belgium to the back of her mind as she leaned against the warmth of his chest.   In her mind's eye they were living for the moment and she was only concerned about the here and now.

A little while later Ken came over to tell him that it was time to leave, since they had to work very early in the morning.

Outside in the parking lot Ken sprawled out on the tarmac while Barbie sat on top of him.

"She doesn't read the Bible huh?"   Steve teased.   "You should take example from her."

Ken got up, lifting Barbie over his head and into the air.

"She's in her very own amusement park," Angel laughed.

"They're made for each other," Steve conceded as he hugged her towards him.

"This is a family thing," Ken said seriously.   "Brother, brother and sister, sister."

At that they all laughed as they made their way to the burger stalls across the street.

Ross drove them to the hotel when they were finsihed eating but after their last experience with the security guard they did not want to take the chance to sneak into the room and stayed in the car instead.

Steve did not want to remain in the car and Angel sympathized with his frustration, considering he was just footsteps away from his room.

"I can't sleep here," Steve complained pushing down Ross's bucket seat with his foot in an effort to make himself comfortable.

"Ken's doing it," she pointed in his brother's direction who was asleep with Barbie on top of him.

With a small note of resignation Steve put his arm around her and tried to do the same.

Before long both brothers were sound asleep and snoring softly while she and Barbie shifted in the confined space.

"He's sweating so much," Barbie said trying to wipe Ken's perspiration away with his shirt collar.

Angel mopped the top of Steve's brow with the back of her hand.   He too was drenched in sweat.

Angel and Barbie on the other hand were enjoying the warmth of the car's interior.   "They're used to living in a fridge while we're accustomed to this tropical heat," Angel mused.

"My temperate baby," Barbie said as she brushed a trickle of sweat away from the tip of Ken's nose.

At the break of dawn, Rodney came knocking on the window of the car.

Angel opened the door a fraction.

"Wake up dem fellas.   They have to go to work," he was smiling as he walked away.

Angel woke up Steve who kissed her before disappearing into his room to get ready. Ken on the other hand was a different story.   He had not budged from his sleeping position and when Barbie's efforts failed, Angel tried to rouse him.

She shook him gently.   "Ken?"

"Ummmm?"   He stirred.

"You have to go to work."

"It's the same as sleeping," he mumbled smiling at her through half closed eyes.

Barbie watched the display of affection between them and thought to herself, it really was a family thing!

Rodney came back by the car.   "You girls are too brave!   Do your parents know where you are?"

"No," they answered truthfully.

"My goodness!"   He shook his head.

"Dem fellas real lucky," he sounded slightly envious.   "Are you going to marry dem?"

"Don't get too far ahead Rodney," Barbie laughed.

"Belgium not like sweet T & T yuh know!   Iz ah a deep freezer over dey!"

Angel rolled her eyes at his rant.

"Well at least you found good guys!"

"How so?"   Barbie was curious.

"I never see dem with nobody. I thought dem was gay.   All de rest have different girls every night!"

"Really?"   Angel asked amused.

"Really!   Doh talk for Abdullah!!   He does have about ten ah night!"

"Who is Abdullah?" They both asked.

"He's from Belgium too but of Turkish descent. And dem Trini girls love him! I surprise all yuh doh know him!"

They both shrugged their shoulders.

Rodney walked away as Steve came over to the car.

"I'm leaving now," he brushed his lips against Angels's.

She smiled as she watched him walk over to the maxi.

"Why can't Ken be like Steve?"   Barbie whined as she waved to him.   He had not bothered to come over to the car.

CHAPTER 7

"I've got a favor to ask."

Dainne raised inquiring brows.

"Can we spend next weekend by you?"

"Just so you can meet them?   No way!"

"Why not?   The boss, now said that due to Carnival we don't have to work.   It's the perfect opportunity."

"No!   No!   No!   Look at you, you're practically skin and bones.   The circles around your eyes are getting darker.   How do you think you're going to look after you wake up how many nights just to go clubbing with them!"

Angel remained silent, she knew Dianne was just concerned for her well being.

"If you collapse do you think they're gonna care?   And who will they call?   Do they know your parents?   Do they even know my number?   No!"   She exploded.   "You're killing yourself for nothing!"

"You don't understand, I'm filling a void."

"You're not listening to me. Brad is gone and they are going, going, gone.   Get that through your head.   You're only going to have a bigger void when they leave."

"I don't care."

"Gosh you're like a brick wall. Thicker than concrete!"   Dianne was losing her patience.

"You know she's too stubborn to change her mind!"   Tammy laughed at Dianne's efforts to dissuade her.

"If anything happens, don't say I didn't warn you," she had a resigned note in her tone now.

"Nothing's going to happen.   Everything will be fine," Angel assured her.

*****

They stood beside the DJ enjoying the music and cool aircondition.   Steve and Ken showed up first, followed by the rest of the group.   He brushed her lips before taking her in his arms and holding her close against him, something she was getting too accustomed with for her own good.

Barbie feeling dejected because Ken had resorted to the opposite end of the club and wasn't paying her any attention, sat down with a thump on the bar stool.   She eyed Angel and Steve with slight envy.   They were so romantic.   Steve was staring down at her sister lovingly and she was looking up at him with adoring eyes as they swayed to the music.

After a while they came over to where she was sitting.

"We're just going outside for a bit," Angel informed.   "Are you okay?"

She nodded as she watched them leave, hand in hand.

They sat down on their usual spot on the bench.

"See how many sores from work," he showed her the palm of his hands.

She touched them gently.   "Kiss them and make them better?"   She asked playfully as she raised one palm to her lips.

"Then you'll have to do the next one too," he teased.

He explained how hard his work was before kissing her and then trailing kisses along her neck.

"It's...wrong," she protested.

"Is it wrong when two people love each other?"   He questioned.

"No," she answered softly.

A small silence passed between them.

"Do you love me?"   She asked meeting his blue eyes.

He nodded, his eyes penetrating hers.

She closed her eyes and pressed her lips against his, knowing with all her heart that she loved him too.   She hadn't fallen head over heals with him in an instant like in the books and movies but she had grown to love him.   To love his affection, his gentle nature, his kind heart, his soft touch, his warm embrace, his loving kisses.   She had grown to love everything about him.

Hand in hand, they returned to the club only to find her sister being entertained by no other than Abdullah.   They were sitting close together and he seemed to have her undevided attention.

Angel's eyes wavered over the room in search of Ken but he was no where to be found.

"I'm so tired," Steve kissed her neck.

Angel sympathized with him.   "Do you want to come to Marabella with us?"   They had the appartment to themselves becuase Dianne was spending the Carnival weekend with her in laws.

Steve nodded.

Barbie was hesitant to leave, wanting to spend more time with Abdullah but Angel didn't take the chance to leave her behind with him.

At the appartment they lay down on the center of the bed.   Steve held her close, kissing her until he fell asleep.   She remained awake for a bit longer before falling asleep too.

Accustomd to rising early, she was the first to awake and sat up on the bed.   Steve stirred next to her and she stared down at him just when his eyes fluttered open.

"Did I wake you?"

"Nope."

"How did you sleep?"

"Good," he half smiled, rising to rest his head on her lap.

She ran her fingers through his hair.

"It's hot in here," he motioned to the sweat on his forehead and she mopped it away with the back of her hand.

"Can I take it off?"   He gestured towards his T-shirt which was clinging to his skin.

She nodded, watching as he pulled it over his head, before discarding it at his foot.

Her eyes travelled over the smooth expanse of his chest and she could not resist the temptation.   She had to touch him, her fingers playing with the fine blond hairs on his chest.

"Is it time for you to go to work?"   She questioned reluctantly.

"What time is it?"

"She turned on the TV to see what time was on the screen.   "Just after seven."

"Oh there's time," he laughed as he gently pulled her down next to him before kissing her passionately.

His hand leafed its way under her blouse to caressivly run up her back, making her body respond with involuntary shivers.   Her body had a mind of its own and impulses and sensations she never thought she was capable of feeling riveted throughout her entire being. He held her closer and she could feel his heart beat against her chest.

They were moving too fast and Angel knew at this rate, if they continued for a minute longer, neither would be able to contain themselves.

"This...is wrong," it took great effort to find her voice and choke out the words.

A moan of frustration escaped his lips.

When their breathing finally returned to normal, Angel murmured against his lips. "I'm sorry."

"You have nothing to be sorry about," he squeezed her affectionately.

He kissed her passionately one more time before getting up to put on his T-shirt.

Angel walked with him to the main street to get a taxi back to the Royal Hotel.

"Black Rose might be playing tonight at Hi-Rpm," he told her.

"Will you be there?"

"If I don't have to work."

A taxi stopped in front them at that point.

"See you tonight?" His eyes were hopeful.

She nodded as he brushed his lips agaisnt hers.

*****

Curtis and other members from Black Rose were on the steps when they arrived. The club was more crowded because it was Carnival Sunday and for some reason it was more fun this time around.

Steve and Ken were more tipsy than usual as they cheered on Black Rose. Three bands played but like always Black Rose topped the cake with their performance.

Steve and Angel went downstairs for fresh air and their traditonal chat when the DJ resumed playing.

"I wish you didn't have to leave so soon."

"I wish I had met you earlier."

She was silently thinking that they had to meet exactly when they did. Nothing before and nothing after. Nothing happens before time - it was an old saying that she still believed in.

"When you love someone it's forever though," he continued.

She nodded, tracing the outline of the scar on his arm before touching the one beneath his chin.

"Do you have any hidden scars?" Her dark eyes met his blue pair.

"Do you mean in my heart?"

She nodded.

"One and when I go back two."

Angel remained silent.

"I've got a big heart that's why I can love both of you.   If I had a small heart I wouldn't be able to do that," he explained.

Then she must have a small heart, she thought because she was capable of loving only one person at a time.

"Then you can go somewhere else and fall in love again?"   It was more a statement than a question.

"I've been around the world, to many different countries but I've never fallen in love until now."

That revelation however did not reassure her.

"In some ways you remind me of her," he continued.

Angel said nothing.

"Sometimes we're close and sometimes we're not," he admitted.

But we're always close.   Why can't you see that?   She screamed internally but didn't say. Instead she pressed her head against his forehead.   "She'll have more of you than I ever will," she finished sadly.

Some time later they returned upstairs to join the group until closing time.   A taxi took them to a bar in San Fernando.   The guys got Carib Beer for themselves and the traditonal Malta for she and Barbie before they all sat outside to chill for a bit.

"We're walking to the hotel," Steve informed her.

"Walking!"

He laughed at her surprised reaction.

"How far is it?"

"Ten miles," he teased before placing his arms around her waist.   Together they half danced through the streets with the group.

It was Jouvert morning and there were huge DJ boxes posted almost every where blasting the latest soca tunes.   Angel couldn't believe that they were actually parading through the streets on Carnival Monday morning like tourists, so much so that a local man offered to

56

show them how it was done.

Two local girls passed by in full Carnival costume and Ken turned back to watch them only to run headlong into a telephone post. Steve, Angel and Barbie almost toppled over with laughter.

"That's a fat post," he stumbled backwards. "They're not normally so fat," he said shaking his head.

The threesome still couldn't catch their breath.

When they finally arrived at the hotel, everyone lowered their voices to hushed tones. Olivier, Mitus and Tall John passed through the front to distract the guards while the rest of them sneaked through the bushes. It was so adventurous, they had to suppress the surge of excitement that made them want to squeal.

Olivier gave them the okay to move forward and Ken proceeded up the stairs to his room, holding Barbie's hand while she and Steve slipped into his on the ground floor.

*****

The next mroning they had breakfast at Mc Donald's in San Fernando.

Nick, one of the workers sat down to join them. Angel knew him because they had done a creative writing course the summer before.

He showed them countless poems he had written, which Angel found were considerably good.

She didn't write poems though. Someone once told her that in order to write poems you had to be self absorbed but to write books you had to love humanity which she did.

"You know what you two girls need?"

"What?" Barbie asked.

"Two good boyfriends!" He teased. "That way you'll stay nice and cosy in bed instead of out here so early in the morning."

CHAPTER 8

"Every Friday you girls want to go clubbing? Not in this house!" Their mother was furious.

"Come on mum," Barbie insisted.

"Maybe next week but not tonight," their mother stated flatly.

Next week might be too late. Things were so uncertain because they could leave any day without notice and all they wanted was to maximise the limited time they had left.

"I'm sure dad will be more understanding!"   Barbie exclaimed before storming out of the kitchen.

Angel stared at her mother wanting to say a whole lot but because too much emotion was stirring beneath the surface, she just turned and walked away.

"You wouldn't believe!"

"Believe what?"   Angel asked popping her head around the shower stall glass so she could see her sister.

"They're letting us go."

"Are you serious?"   Angel was uncertain.

"I am, so hurry up so I can shower!"   Barbie urged.

Angel stared through the window of the maxi, trying not to think of all that had transpired.

"Can I ask you something?"   Barbie spoke softly.

"Sure," she replied in a distant tone.

"If Brad wanted you back would you take him?"

Angel didn't have to think about it.   "No," she answered with certainty.   "Why do you ask?" She turned towards Barbie.

Her sister looked away guiltily.   "I have a confession to make..."

"Before we left for Marabella that first time, Brad had called."

"He did?"   Angel was confused.

" I got the call but I told him that you didn't want to speak to him and then I slammed down the phone."

Angel remained silent with an unreadable expression which made Barbie uncertain.

"Are you angry that I did?"

"No," Angel answered honestly.

She was thinking that as the saying goes every thing happened for a reason.   Had she taken the call she might have forgiven Brad and made the biggest mistake of her life by marrying him. She would have never met Steve or found true love.

Living for a Moment

*****

He kissed her passionately as they sat on the bench outside the mall.

"Why don't you live a little?"   His blue eyes were burning with desire.

She didn't need to sleep with him to live a little she thought.   If he only knew all the sacrifices she made   just to be there with him, he wouldn't say that but she didn't let him know.

"Doesn't everything make you think of a movie or a romance novel?"   She questioned instead.

He shook his head to say no.

To her it was all surreal.   He probably could not see it that way because he had travelled the world but she was just an island girl who had never been out of the country.   To find love in the arms of someone from half way across the world was dreamlike to her.

"Do you believe that dreams come true?"

He nodded

She pressed her lips against his.   In her heart of hearts he was her dream come true.

"Yhan told me that you're his best friend but he hates you because you don't tell him anything that goes on between us," she laughed.   With Yhan everything was comical.

"He does not need to know."

*****

The group piled into the maxi from the Royal Hotel as they headed en route to Maracas.   Her sister was sitting behind with Abdullah who was stopping off at Piarco International Airport, Steve was sitting beside her handing out Carib beer from the cooler while Ken and Yhan were sitting infront them.   Yhan's father was sitting next to the driver while Tall John was sitting with the girl he had met a few nights before in the back seat.   Angel didn't know her name yet but supposed everyone would get aquainted at the beach.

She was in Trinidad but she could have very well been in a different country because the landscape was alien to her and as the maxi cruized over the highway, she was filled with a sense of anticipation and adventure.   It was after eight in the morning and they were heading North when they were supposed to be home by nine, deep down South.   Their parents were going to kill them, she mused.

Yhan started singing loudly.   "Three by three is nine Angel sing your song this time!" He bellowed.

Angel turned to Steve in rescue.

"You don't have to sing if you don't want to," Steve assured her.

59

Yhan then stretched out his foot, allowing his toes to wriggle by the driver's ear. Everyone started laughing at his antics. Angel was seriously thinking that he had some loose screws.

"Is it always so much fun?" She questioned Steve.

"Sometimes it's more."

Angel could not remember when last she had this much fun.

Steve stretched out on the seat, resting his head on her lap and she stroked his face, allowing his stubble to graze against her hand and enjoying the feel of it. He didn't like to shave for whatever reason but she didn't have a problem with that. He could go bald like Yhan or grow his hair to the floor and it wouldn't make a difference because he would still be Steve to her and his appearance didn't change the way she felt about him. She wouldn't trade him for any guy in the maxi, nor would she trade him for another man in the world.

She looked down to find his blue eyes staring up at her and she absently wondered what he was thinking. She didn't ask but smiled with him instead. He sent her a kiss in the air before closing his eyes and drifting off to sleep.

Yhan was still doing amusing stuff and she couldn't help thinking that he would make a superb comedian. Angel tilted her head backwards to see what her sister was up to and found her sitting on Abdullah's lap. They were staring into each other's eyes with so much emotion that Angel was taken aback because they hardly knew each other, but their bond was obviously intense.

Finally they arrived at the airport and everyone jumped out to explore, browsing through the souvenir shops and taking photos next to the Carnival displays like tourists. Forming a circle around Abdullah and her sister, the group watched as they hugged and kissed passionately for the last time.

A local X rated magazine circulated through the group and Angel obliviously reached for it to check out her horoscope but Yhan wouldn't allow her to see it as he playfully kept it from her.

"I'll read it for you," he insisted. "Today you're going to Maracas. You and Steve are going to kiss and a little more..." he paused making eveyone laugh. "In Trinidad Steve is good but in Belgium he is better! Steve is going to marry you and take you back to Belgium with him!"

At that, the group cheered loudly. Angel's eyes flickered uncertainly to Steve to see his reaction. He had a faraway look in his eyes that she didn't want to dwell on. Yhan closed the magazine and then everyone waved goodbye to Abdullah before really starting on their journey to Maracas.

Steve resumed his position on her lap and she absently ran her fingers through his hair.

Yahn stopped the maxi in the middle of the highway. "Typical piss stop!" He shouted, making everyone laugh as he got out to relieve himself and before he could get back in he fell flat on his face.   Again everyone toppled over with laughter.

Before long the maxi diverted from the highway and the scenery changed drastically into forestry as they followed the narrow road which meandered upwards, seemingly forever.   The picturesque landscape was breathtaking and the sight of Trinidad in the valley below left her mesmerised.   It was hard to believe that she had lived in Trinidad all her life and had never been up there until now.

When she finally set eyes on the blue green water below, she was filled with a reverential sense of wonder that even surprised Steve.   As the maxi descended, a surge of excitement filled her veins and she couldn't wait for them to reach their destination.   The feeling of exhilaration was a refreshing new experience for her and she savored every minute.

At long last the maxi pulled into the car park and everyone rushed out.   Angel and Barbie hugged each other, surpressing the urge to squeal in delight.

Steve took her hand before leading her over to one of the breakfast stalls for bake and shark and even that was a new experience for her.

After eating she watched as he spread one of the hotel's blanket on the sand before gently drawing her down next to him to apply sun tan lotion on her back.   The feel of his strong hands against her skin reduced her defenses.   Her body relaxed at his touch and she was silently amazed at how good the message felt.   The tension in her muscles ebbed away as he gently rubbed the lotion in.

"I'll give you a proper massage when we get back to the hotel," he said huskily as he raised her up from the blanket playfully.   Hand in hand they walked towards the water, the soft white sand hot beneath their feet.

The salty sea air felt wonderful against her face as they stepped into the water.

Angel squealed in delight making Steve laugh.   Barbie joined them squealing as well.

They watched as Steve and Ken swam into the deep, while they stayed close to the shore.   The North Coast current was so strong, that the breaking waves threw them over as it came crashing over their heads.   They spluttered and coughed the saltly water out of their lungs before returning on the blankets to dry off in the sun.   The entire group did pretty much the same and before long everyone was sprawled out sun bathing.

Steve placed his head on her lap and she absently played with his hair as she stared out at the ocean.   Her mind, used to trailing away now reflected on the night before.   She couldn't stop herself from smiling as she remembered how they sneaked through the bushes like two teenagers to lie on the grass of the hotel's grounds.   She remembered the serene feeling of lying next to him under the open sky in the velvet black of night.   There had been a full moon and to her there was nothing more romantic than a full moon. The moonlight had filtered through the branches of the huge trees that towered above them, illuminating their faces as they kissed while an owl hooted somewhere in the distance.

Some tourists talking near by drew her thoughts back to the present.   Steve had fallen asleep and she gently placed his head on the blanket so she could get up and stretch her legs. Ken stirred on the blanket next to them and she moved away not wanting to wake him.   Ken the younger of the brothers was as introverted as her, she thought as she joined Barbie who was sitting closer to the water.

"Thinking about Abdullah?"   Angel teased.

Barbie smiled.   "He's in the air now."

"I'm still not used to the idea of you and him," Angel admitted.

Barbie shrugged her shoulders. "We understand each other."

"The tide is coming up, we need to wake those fellas."

Everyone moved away, except for Yhan who wouldn't budge from his sleep.   After a while he got up and stared around confused before falling flat on his face again. Everyone laughed.   Yhan was just too comical for anyone to take seriously.

"He has five older sisters," Steve told Angel still laughing.

"Really!   He's the only guy?"

"He was a mistake," Steve laughed drawing her down on the blanket next to him.

Steve kissed her belly button playfully before biting her.

A giggle of surprise escaped her lips.

"I want to eat you," he mumbled against her skin.

If you were my husband you could devour every part of me, she thought but didn't say.

"How do you say hello in Flemish?"   She questioned.

"Hallo."

"And good morning?"

"Guten Morgen."

"It's not so different," she commented.

"For those two it's not but for the rest of the language it is," he playfully kissed her fingers as he stared at her.

Yhan who had finally gotten up came over to where they were, singing **Butterfly by Crazy**

Town.

He called Steve 'Sugar'and Steve called him 'Baby'and she couldn't resist laughing.

"Do you know the part in the song that says, *I used to think that happy endings were only in the books I read but you made me feel alive when I was almost dead*?"

He shook his head in denial.

She said nothing but that was the part of the song that she could relate to, because that was how he made her feel.

"You like to write?"   He asked breaking into her thoughts.

She nodded.

"Maybe you should write a book about us.   It might be a bestseller," he smiled.

"It's not going to have a happy ending though."

"You mean because I'm going back?"

She nodded.

"Not every book have happy endings."

Touche, she thought to herself.   It was not like she was oblivious of that.   She didn't say anything and silently tried to be unmoved by his insensitive statement.   It made her think and not for the first time that she was just a substitute for his girlfriend back in Belgium.   She was just the person who was conveniently available until he returned.   She was quiet but not stupid.   She knew all that and yet it did not matter.

She stared down at him, he had fallen asleep again with his head on her lap and she traced the outline of his face with her fingers thinking that you never knew what you were missing until it arrived.   How did someone hold on to something they've always wanted when it was finally dilivered?   She could not answer her own question.   She stared down at him and wished time could just suspend in mid air.   Everything felt like a wonderful dream she didn't want to wake up from.   Love finds you when you least expect it, she had read somewhere.   That was something she never believed until now.   Tammy once said to her that sometimes God lets us meet a few wrong people before finding the right one.   She had found her Mr. Right, only he didn't belong to her.   The irony of life, she thought.

Placing his head on the blanket once more, she got up to walk a bit.   She guessed it was better to experience the pain of heartache than to never find love, but figured that was just the romantic side of her talking.   She walked towards the shoreline, letting the cool water ripple through her toes as she stared out at the aquamarine ocean.   She inhaled deeply as her mind absorbed everything.   She was never going to forget today, for as long as she lived.

As the sun changed position in the sky, she retuned to where Steve was.   She looked down at this man and couldn't believe how much she loved him.   She loved him more than she thought she could love another human being - with her heart, mind, body and soul.   He had said that he loved her too and she believed him but he didn't love her enough to stay or take her back with him.   She loved him with her entire heart, while part of his heart belonged to someone else.   She knew all this and still it made no difference because they were living for the moment.

With that thought in mind, she lay down next to him and closed her eyes, listening to the healthy roar of the ocean echoing in her ears.   She thought of how small and insignificant they all were on the earth in comparison to the sky above them or the sand beneath them. Everything was out of her hands and she left it up to providence as she drifted off to sleep.

CHAPTER 9

"Hi, how are you?" Britney asked cheerfully as she hugged Angel.   "Where's your sister?"

"She went to the restroom, she'll be out shortly.   How are you?"   Angel returned politely.

"I'm good. I spent all week with John at the hotel, cherishing each moment."

"That's nice," Angel was sincere.   She hardly knew Britney but so far she seemed genuine.

"It's going to be so hard now that they're leaving next week."

"They're leaving next week?"   Angel tried to keep the surprise out of her voice.

"Aye," she continued in her British accent.

"Who?"

"John, Steve and Yhan."

Even though she had known the inevitable departure would reach eventually, Angel had avoided thinking about it and now that it had creeped up upon her, she was totally unprepared.

"Which day of next week?"   Her voice quivered slightly.

"Tuesday," Britney answered between a puff of cigarette.

That was only three days away and Angel could almost hear the clock ticking in her head. Pretty soon it was going to be time to say goodbye and she silently dreaded the event.

"Their boss had a bar-b-cue for them at his house today and John called me and said that they'll all be at Tree House tonight.   Do you want to come?"   Her eyes were eager.

"Where is that?"

"It's in St. Joseph."

"I don't know it," Angel admitted.

"But I do.   We can meet them there because I doubt that they'll come here tonight."

Angel nodded.   She knew that if she didn't see Steve tonight, she might never see him again.

"Hi there!"   Britney greeted Barbie on arrival, also hugging her.   "I was just telling your sister that we can meet the guys at Tree House."

Barbie had a perplexed expression in her eyes.

"Steve is leaving next week," Angel informed, observing as her bewilderment changed to shock.

"Next week!   Is Ken leaving too?"   She couldn't help asking.

"I don't know.   John didn't say," Britney answered uncertainly.

For a split second everyone was silent.

"So are you girls up for it or not?"   Britney asked, sounding slightly impatient.

"Yes," they both said in unison.

By the time they arrived at Tree House Angel had recovered from her initial shock and was more prepared to face them.   The first familiar face she recognized was Ken and hugging him around his waist she asked for Steve.

"Steve?   Who's Steve?"   He teased, making her smile in spite of everything.

Before Ken got a chance to point him out, Angel saw him, slightly noting his funky hair cut as she walked over.

"Hi," she greeted him.

"Hi yourself," he seemed really surprised to see her.

"How did you get here?"

Angel motioned with her hand in Britney's direction, who was already sitting comfortable on top of tall John's lap.

"I've got some bad news," he wasted no time in beating around the bush. "I'm leaving next week."

"I know," she said motioning to Britney again and noticing at the same time that he didn't even look disturbed. He was all happy go lucky.

"Would you like something to drink?"

"No," she answered, hardly in the mood for anything.

"Well if you want anything just ask."

How about, don't leave? She thought before mentally shaking herself.

He ordered her traditional Malta before leaving to use to restroom and Angel fitted herself against the counter in the space he had just vacated. Her eyes waved around the room blindly as she sipped her drink feeling neither here nor there. She was somewhat suspended in mid air.

"You look sad," he said stopping infront her on his return.

How do you expect me to be? You're leaving in three days! Her mind screamed.

"I always look sad," she said instead.

"You look sadder tonight," he insisted but she said nothing.

"You knew though   It's no surprise because you knew from the start that this was going to happen."

Angel watched him and wondered how he could be so insensitive at a time like this. Of course she knew but that didn't deminish the hurt she was feeling now. In a normal situation she wouldn't tolerate such insensitivity but this wasn't a normal situation. This wasn't just a random person. This was Steve, the man she loved. Her one exception.

"At the back of my mind I knew the day was going to come sooner or later but I avoided thinking about it until now. The next time someone from far away comes, don't get involved because you're only going to get hurt."

She didn't answer but thought someone else might love her enough to stay. Someone else wouldn't love her then leave. Angel surpressed the tears. Blinking she looked away to find Ken's eyes on her. He was staring at her in the way she wished Steve would. His blue eyes were filled with so much emotion and so much concern that she tried to smile to let him know that she was okay but her lips were quivering so much that she couldn't pull it off.

Turning away from Ken she reached out for Steve, pulling him towards her.

"I want to hold you," her voice was emotional as she buried her face in his chest, not sure of how he would respond but he enveloped her in his arms in the way that she cherished and it took all she had not to break down.

Ken made an effort to take a picture of them holding each other but other people were more eager, rendering his efforts futile.   Angel reflected that it was probably for the best. She didn't think that Steve would want his girlfriend finding a picture of them in such a loving embrace.   Not that Ken would reveal their picture anyway.

"Where do you want to go?   Hi-Rpm or the hotel?"   Steve aked after a while.

"I don't know.   What do you want?"

"Tonight you're the queen.   You're the queen of my heart.   Whatever you decide, we'll do."

"The hotel."   She didn't want their last night to be in a nightclub surrounded by loud music and strangers.   She wanted them to spend quality time together.

"Then the hotel it is," he said holding her hand as they followed the group out.

On the steps outside Ken tried again to take a picture of them only to realize he was out of films much to his dismay.

Angel smiled at his efforts.   The gesture was very sweet.

At the hotel Angel settled against the pillows listening to music on his Discman while he showered.   He joined her shortly after, turning off the lamps and pulling her towards him before kissing her passionately.   Angel responded with the same fevor.

He trailed kisses along her neck, his hands caressivly burning her skin.   Before she could even register what was happening, his weight was pinning her down.   She could feel his heart throbbing against her as they continued to kiss passionately.

Her entire body was yielding to him against her will, every fibre of her being at his mercy.

"Please...be..a good guy..."

A small moan of frustration escaped his lips.

"I'm always a good guy," he dropped his head against her breasts in frustration.

"Why?" He asked at last.

"Because I want my first time to be with my husband, not with someone who's leaving me...but I do love you..."

He gently rolled off her before hugging her towards him.   "I love you too," he kissed her neck.

Shortly after he fell asleep but Angel remained awake, watching him in the darkness as her tears burned the pillow. Tonight was going to be the last night to sleep in his arms. The last night that they would be together and she cried long and hard, her sobs echoing in the darkness. She cried for all the happy days they shared that were never coming back and for the happy days in the future that they would never know. She cried not understanding why something so good had to end.

With a trembling finger she traced the outline of his face, along the masculine curve of his jaw before running her index finger caressively over his lips. She pressed her lips lightly against his, tasting the salt from her own tears, before kissing the bridge of his nose and then his sleeping eyelids. Finally she pressed her lips against his forehead.

"I love you Steve," she murmured against his warm skin. "More than you will ever know."

With her head pressed against his, she closed her eyes and alllowed herself to drift off into a light sleep but before she knew it, Rodney was knocking at the door. It was time to leave.

"I hate goodbyes," Steve said as he kissed her.

She was lying on top his chest, staring down at him as he stared lovingly up at her, his palm caressing the side of her face.

"Me too," she smiled down at him.

Barbie opened the door. "We have to leave," she urged.

Steve kissed her again and Angel slipped a picture of him, her and Ken on his bedside cabinet. He was probably going to leave it for the cleaning lady to discard but a small part of her hoped he would keep it as a token to remind him of their time spent together. In the photo Ken was hugging her, not him so there was nothing for his girlfriend to be suspicious of, if she stumbled upon it.

Kissing him one last time, she left to join Barbie who was standing outside with Rodney.

"I have to hand it to you girls, you're very brave!"

"You think?" Barbie teased.

"Very brave! Last night you just walked in like you owned the place eh! Never bothered to check fuh meh!"

"Pretty soon you won't have to deal with that agian."

"How so?"

"The guys are leaving so you won't be seeing us again."

68

"Oh..."   He sounded disappointed.   "Will you girls write?"

"Sure Rodney, we'll write to you!"   Barbie teased.

CHAPTER 10

Angel was sitting next to Yhan in the hotel's lobby, enjoying his sense of humour.   Even on a dispiriting day like the present he still had the ability to make her laugh.

"I've got to show you something," Yhan said drawing her closer to look inside his bag.   He had stolen the hotel's bible.

"I had to take it," he insisted, making her laugh.

"Are you going to read it?"   She asked curiously.

He nodded.

Steve offered them something to drink but they refused.

"So what, we're not good anymore?"   Yhan questioned.   "We'll go and sit on the next table," he gestured to the far corner.

Angel pushed his shoulder playfully.   "You know we don't want that."

He smiled with her.

"What are you going to do when you get back?"   She was trying to keep herself distracted with Yhan so she wouldn't have to look at Steve who was sitting detached from the group.

"I'm going to drink a few Caribs with my daddy and then I'm going to visit my grandmother.   I love my grandmother!"

"That's sweet," Angel commented.

"Manoor threw up after trying to drink as much as us at Tree House last night!"

"Really?"

Yhan nodded seriously.   "In Belgium his name means manwhore," Yahn continued.

Angel stared at him with a bewildered expression.

"You know a whore? Well man whore!"   He explained making her laugh.

"Will he be sober enough to drive you guys to the airport?"

"I hope so!"   Yhan laughed.

"Steve is sad," Barbie whispered next to her but Angel pretended not to hear.   She was not ready to look at him.

"Steve it wouldn't make you less of a man if you cried," Britney commented.

Her words drew Angel's attention and she raised her eyes to study him.   He was clearly fighting back his emotions and losing the battle big time.   When his blue eyes met hers all she saw was raw emotion.

Sad eyes never lie by Enrique Iglesias popped into her head.   The eyes were really the windows to our soul she thought, for in that instant she read him like an open book through his eyes. Her heart twisted in her chest as the reality of it all kicked in from that one look.   This was really goodbye.

She walked over with wobbly legs, to sit on his lap as she put her arms around him. He held her back.   They held on to each other without saying anything.   Angel lost all sense of time as they clung to each other until Manoor pulled up with the maxi.   The same maxi that had taken them to Maracas not long ago.   With heavy hearts they boarded the maxi for the last time.

Angel touched his face knowing that she was never going to feel his stubble graze against her skin again.

Yhan who was sitting in the seat in front them, turned around to stare at them.

"That's the last time you're going to touch his beard," he said as if reading her mind.

"I know," she answered sadly

"You love his beard?"   Yhan teased.

"I love everything about him," she responded making Yhan smile.

"You're leaving him."

"No.   He's leaving me."

Steve remained silent next to her, unsmiling and withdrawn.   She could feel him shutting her out and there was nothing she could do about it.   He wasn't even in Belgium yet but Angel could feel the ocean between them already.

"We're here," he said in a horse whisper when the maxi finally pulled up at Piarco International Airport.

The last time they had been there Angel had been eager to jump out and explore but at the very moment she was reluctant to come out the maxi.

They checked in before eveyone sat outside on the wooden benches, soaking in the tropical sun as the departure time ticked on.

"Cheer up!   At least we're out of Royal Prison!"   Tall John tried to lighten the mood but everyone was too despondent to smile.

Steve showed Angel his passport photo of him with long hair.

"You look the same," she smiled up at him.   His head was clean shaven now but he was still her Steve, with or without hair.

"It's time," Tall John announced flatly and they all made their way over to the departure gate.

Angel hugged Yhan first because unlike Steve, he still felt human.   He still had blood flowing through his veins and she could feel his warmth as he embraced her.

When Steve held her after, it made her think of an emotionless German soilder, he had ice flowing through his veins.   She could not feel him at all.   Only his yes couldn't lie.   The blue depths were as greived as her own.

She had read somewhere that when you loved someone you had to let them go and if that love was true then they would come back to you.   Well she was letting him go but she knew he was never coming back to her.

They hugged each other one last time.

"Take care of yourself," they said in unison but neither smiled at the coincidence.

The threesome watched as the other three went through the departure gates.   Tall John looked over his shoulder to wave at Britney and Yhan turned around to watch them one last time but Steve never looked back.   He kept walking, giving Angel nothing to hold on to.   His name rose up her throat but died on her lips as she watched him go.

Angel stared through the window at the brown cane fields as the taxi drove them away from the airport.   She stared at the fields without really seeing them.   She wasn't going to cry, she decided as she tried to focus on the happy times they had together.   Then *Lifehouse* song *Hanging by a moment* started playing and all the memories flooded in.

At the end of the song Emmet Henessy, the radio anouncer said," And the moment is over!"

His words were the straw that broke her as the tears spilled from her eyes in endless streams down her face.

*****

Angel followed Tammy to stand on the veranda of the office building.

"How are you holding up?"   She questioned with concern.

"Okay, I guess," Angel shrugged her shoulders.

"But you knew from the beginning this was going to happen."

"Don't remind me," Angel rolled her eyes as she toyed with the lapels of her jacket.

"Do you have any regrets?"   Tammy had to ask.

"No."

A pregnant pause decended upon them.

"What are you thinking?"   Tammy probed gently.

"Can someone really love two persons at the same time?"

"It happens every day," Tammy consoled her.

*****

"I saw Britney today," Barbie informed.

"Oh?"

"She said Tall John phoned her to let her know that he posted Belgian chocolates for her birthday."

"That's nice," Angel commented.

"She said that he told her Yhan was his usual comical self on the flight over to Belgium but Steve did not say one word during the entire flight.   He just had his headphones on the whole time but he looked like he was struggling to hold it together."

Angel remained silent.

"He really did love you.   You know that?"   Barbie searched her face.

Angel shrugged her shoulders.   She didn't know anything, anymore.

*****

Angel headed to Pennywise Cosmetics, a popular shop in town, in search of something to remind her of Steve.   She wanted something to make her know that he was real and not just a depiction in her imagination.

72

Slowly she walked over to the male counter line.   She knew exactly what she was looking for and when she saw it, she pointed it out to the sales clerk.

"The musk aftershave in the black bottle."

The sales clerk placed it on the counter.

"Can I open it?"

The other nodded and Angel removed the cap and placed the bottle under her nostrils.   She inhaled deeply as the smell of Steve invaded her senses.   It was so strong that he could have been standing next to her.

"I'll take it," she said huskily.

Sitting at her desk later that evening, she splashed some of the aftershave on her wrists. Inhaling the aroma of Steve and remembering his presence she took out a few pages and her pen.   She was going to write the book Steve wanted her to write.   Maybe years from now when she published it, he might stumble upon it in some book store half way across the world and come to realise just how much she loved him.

Scrawling across the top of the page she wrote the title of the book -

Living For a Moment.

Living for a Moment